Fall in love
with me

WILLOW WINTERS

Fall in love
with me

xoxo Kelz

Prologue

Aubrey

"I COULD LIE HERE FOREVER." I'M BARELY able to murmur the words. Naked and sated, enveloped in warmth and comforted by his strong arm, holding me close to him. As if he'd need to hold me there to keep me close. My body molds to his easily, comfortably, as if this is where I've always belonged.

There's a hint of a gruff inhale, one tinged with the masculine approval of a deep rumble. Instantly, a simper pulls at my lips.

"If that's what you want," he decides. He smirks down at me before turning on his side and lifting the sheet to hover over me.

He buries his head in the crook of my neck,

leaving openmouthed kisses and letting his stubble tickle along my tender skin. My body bows on its own and my head pushes into the plush pillow as I let out a small laugh. With my palms weakly pressing against his hard chest, he nips my neck and I let out a gasp. Every nerve ending in my body lights on fire, all of that pleasure coming back to the surface, but exhaustion holds me back … that and something else.

"You wore me out," I protest with a smile and peer up at him. I'm caught in his gaze, in a way I don't expect, in a way that sears my soul.

It was just a fling, it was just fun, but as my heart races and my blood heats, I can't deny it's something else now. Something more. Something that feels like it was meant to be. Like I always belonged to him and he to me.

"Will you hold me, though?" I whisper and there's something so delicate, so easily broken between us. A moment passes and I'm far too aware of the fragility of it all.

I love this man. I love him and he could so easily break my heart. Is it rare to know the moment? To have such certainty? The moment I begin to question it, Bennet brushes the tip of his nose against mine and then closes his eyes, resting his forehead against mine as he kisses my lips.

It all happens far too quickly before he says, "Of course I will, my sweetheart."

I know then for sure, as the bed groans and he settles in beside me … very much more awake than I was a moment ago, this man took my heart. His to have and his to break. I didn't give it to him. Not with conscious consent.

With one last kiss, he tells me to sleep well and to dream of him. All the while I can barely breathe with the realization. How did it happen so quickly?

How the hell did I let that happen at all?

chapter
One

Aubrey

"Miss Peters?" The deep voice I recognize easily from the other side of my front door belongs to Stewart.

With a stripe of hair removal cream on my right leg, my left a bit pink from rubbing it down a moment ago, I carefully make my way to the door, practically hobbling and yell, "Coming!"

It's a small town; everyone knows everyone else and I've known Stew since he was ten years old and his family moved to Cedar Lane from the West Coast.

Cedar Lane is the epitome of East Coast suburbia tucked away in the lower bit of Pennsylvania. It's the perfect location for peace and quiet, although there's always something to gossip about over a cup of coffee on a neighbor's porch.

The leaky pipe in my kitchen isn't one of those things, or at least I didn't think it was … until I open the door. My damp hair falls down my shoulders as I fist my robe, making sure it's closed tight.

"Hey Stew—" My greeting is cut short. Suddenly I'm unable to tell him to come on in and that I'll just be upstairs, staying out of his way.

My heart hammers as pale blue eyes gaze back at me. They're accompanied by rough stubble, and kissable lips I remember all too well.

"You brought help?" I barely get out the words that are stuck in my throat. I will myself to stop staring, but I can't. My heart skips a beat as I recognize a man I haven't seen for years.

"You remember Bennet?" Stew asks me and I choke on a "yup" before clearing my throat and shaking off my rattled nerves.

Bennet Thompson is tall, dark and handsome, with a charming smile that would make any woman's legs weak. "Nice to see you, Miss Peters," he greets me and offers a courteous nod.

I swallow down a lump in my throat and give him a polite reply.

"You too. Thanks so much for coming."

Stewart makes his way in and I have to step to the side. It's then that the scent of the hair removal cream hits me and I realize I've only just gotten out of the shower so my long brunette hair is still wet. Without a drop of makeup on, I'm wearing an old cotton robe and I smell like ... scorched hair.

Closing my eyes, I take a deep, steadying breath. I regret this decision immensely.

Two sets of boots hit the floor and Stew gestures to Bennet, indicating where the kitchen is. Which is what I should be doing. I can't believe he's back in town.

Wearing dark blue jeans, work boots and a simple black tee that hugs those broad shoulders just right, I can't tear my eyes away from the sight of him.

Memories hit me one by one.

Bennet dated my best friend in high school. Pamela moved away a few years ago when a lawyer came into town and swept her off her feet. He stole her away back to his hometown. People rarely come and go once they move here. To see Bennet back, though ... it takes me back to those first moments of puppy love.

To a foolish teen who had a crush on her best

friend's boyfriend. Which was never going to be anything. Even when they broke up, he was off-limits.

… Pamela is married now, though, and with that thought, I inwardly kick myself for not checking to see if Bennet has a ring on his finger.

I close the door, ready to sneak a peek with both men's backs to me as they face the kitchen sink. Stew explains to Bennet the problems I've had with the old plumbing and I'm caught off guard as Stew turns abruptly.

Thankfully he doesn't seem to notice my shock at being caught and I keep my one arm crossed in front of me, the other still clutching my robe.

"If you'll just fill this out when you have a moment," Stew tells me, waving the old clipboard with an attached pen he always carries around. He leaves it on the counter and behind him, Bennet crouches down, opening the doors beneath the sink and disappearing from view.

"I have another call that needs me, but I'm going to leave this paperwork with you," Stew explains. "You're in good hands," Stew adds and then tells Bennet he's leaving. It's at that moment Bennet stands, facing both of us from the other side of the mineral gray granite island.

He runs his hand up the back of his neck and over his hair before giving Stew a wave and saying, "No worries. I can take care of this."

For a moment, I hear him say "her." I can take care of "her" … *Oh yes, I'm sure he could.*

With a heated blush creeping into my cheeks, I scold myself. It doesn't matter that I pined over him for years, we've never been a thing and I'm sure we never will.

chapter
Two

Bennet

IT IS HER. A COLD SWEAT BREAKS OUT ON THE back of my neck as I do my best to act as casual as possible. Like it doesn't get to me to see her again after all these years.

Wrapped in only a thin robe with a look in her eyes that tells me she remembers me just as well as I remember her.

I swear back then, there was a tension between us and I always thought it was because she was off-limits. I thought, maybe I only felt that way because I knew she'd never let me take her out, she'd never kiss me. Not when I had dated her best friend. Even if that never went anywhere. For the rest of high school,

Aubrey was her closest friend and we only ever shared stolen glances.

Glances that made my heart beat faster and sent a tingle of heat down my shoulders. Glances exactly like the one we just had.

It's a small town and Cedar Lane is even smaller. Housewives and busybodies keep the gossip as fresh and hot as the coffee at the corner diner. I wonder why Aubrey picked this place but the answers stare back at me. From the cozy but contemporary furniture, to the rose bushes out front and the picket fence, it's obvious. She's the girl next door in a small town and everything about this place speaks to that.

From the walls painted a soft sage and the accompanying accents in the kitchen, to the walnut floor that matches the cabinetry, this is a home. One with little touches like owl-shaped spatulas and a pitcher of homemade lemonade she put out on the counter. There are even fresh slices of lemons.

It's hard to remain professional and not take in every detail about the girl next door I couldn't have.

"If you'd like a glass, feel free," she says and her comment draws my attention back to her. Right before it moves to the robe she's holding on to tight. Clearing my throat, I thank her.

"I appreciate it," I tell her and don't dare move my gaze from hers. Whatever I do now won't be her first impression of me, but it's my first day of work since I've been home. The first time she's seen me in years. I'm riddled with nervousness riddles, like a lovesick teen.

"Don't mind me, Miss Peters, I'll have this fixed up for you and be gone before you know it," I tell her in as even of a voice as I can manage. Although I nearly pause my statement at her cringe. "It's miss … right?" I ask to clarify and for a moment, for one small moment, I'm anxious.

The very idea of her being married creates a tension in every muscle I have.

With a quick shake of her head and a warm blush rising up through her chest and into her cheeks, she corrects me. "You can call me Aubrey, Bennet."

My name. Her lips.

Fuck me.

There's a silence between us as only our eyes lock and the temperature rises. That blush of hers rises too, all the way up to her temples.

I'm hard instantly. Those doe eyes and that naive innocence about her have always done something to me.

"I'll just be," she starts, her voice coming out in a high pitch and she steps backward, nearly kicking a cardboard box that's damp and out of place. It must have been under the leaky sink when the pipe busted.

"Oh," she says with a gasp, almost falling back, and that robe slips just slightly. As quick as I can, I force my gaze up to the left and turn slightly. Fuck me. That glimpse of her soft curves and that quick peek at her breasts will be burned into my memory forevermore. "Oh my God." The sound of her stumbling over something is comical.

"I didn't see a thing," is all I say although it's not exactly the truth. An asymmetric smirk lifts the corner of my lips up and I hide it by rubbing my hand over my jaw.

Her bare feet pad on the floor as she rushes out that she'll be upstairs if I need her.

My mind wanders back to our past as I work. Back to the fact that her friend asked me out before I could ask Aubrey out. Pamela moved to Denver I think, had two kids and has a great life. I couldn't care less about any of that. The only piece that matters is whether or not that's changed Aubrey's mind about dating me.

I huff a humorless laugh as I work on the busted pipe, cutting it out and doing everything I can to tamp down the feelings racing through me.

Aubrey is settled here, and I've only just come home, taking up this job until I get grounded. There's no way in hell a girl like her would date a rough, blue-collar man like me.

chapter
Three

Aubrey

ALL I CAN IMAGINE IS HIS ROUGH, callused hands on my body. And it is so, so wrong. He's here on business and working. Hell, I'm sure he didn't even know I still existed until he saw me. He probably didn't even remember my name.

Miss Peters. I remember him calling me that and it's like stepping into a cold shower. Until I remember the way he looked at me when I told him to call me Aubrey. And how invested he seemed to be when he asked if I was a "miss."

I bite down on my lower lip to stifle my squeal of delight and smile as I push open one of the two French doors leading to the en suite bathroom.

Bennet Thompson will never know what he does to me. Did to me. I try to correct myself but no, shaking my head I have to admit, he is very much doing it in present tense now.

It's been years since I've really thought of him. I've buried myself in so much work as an editor that I've rarely noticed men at all. One look at Bennet and bam, I turned into a blushing fool.

Flicking the light on, I lean against the sink and try to contain myself.

Never in my life have I felt so … bad. He makes me think about things I shouldn't. Makes me hot when I shouldn't be. *He's only here to fix a broken pipe.*

I can't help the grin and the dirty thoughts that come to mind as I shake off my daydream and get back to the task of pampering myself. Pampering may not be the right word given that my calves are burning. This cream needs to come off right freaking now.

The water rushes out of the faucet as I wipe off the hair remover and go about my normal routine. One glance in the mirror and I cringe. Way to make an impression, I guess. If I had to depict it in a single sentence, I'd describe myself as a mouse who got caught in the rain. In the oversized robe I'm drowning, and my long brunette hair is nearly black because it's still wet and stuck to my flushed skin.

It's not exactly the outfit and styling I'd have chosen for the event that just played out on the first floor of my house. Grimacing, I keep myself firmly focused on the facts. Bennet doesn't want me, he never has and I've probably made a fool of myself.

This reality is certainly not a part of the thoughts that run through my head. Streaming my favorite channel on my phone, I turn the music up and ignore what happened.

Hooking up with Bennet is nothing but a fantasy and one I haven't thought about in years.

And one that most certainly isn't going to come true.

With a firm nod in the mirror, I turn on the blow-dryer and for some unknown reason I make sure my makeup is perfect, complete with a deep red lipstick.

I even take the time to curl my hair. All the while I imagine Bennet will leave the moment he's done.

I've embarrassed myself enough already.

With a pucker of my lips, I hang up my robe and head back to my bedroom to grab a matching set of lingerie I haven't thought of since I bought it with a gift card from one of my friends two holidays ago.

I only make it a few steps before I turn to the door. I swear I heard a knock over the music, still blaring, and before I can answer, the door opens. Obviously on its own from the gentle push of a knock. I hadn't shut it all the way.

My heart pounds as I screech out "one minute," with one arm wrapped around my chest, the other down low to cover my hoo-ha, but it's all too late.

In the blink of an eye … well, Bennet got an eye-ful. Making those gorgeous pale blue eyes of his as wide as I've ever seen them as he chaotically reaches for the doorknob to slam the door shut tight.

…

Oh my God, how did this just get worse?

chapter
Four

Bennet

TWO THOUGHTS ENTER MY MIND ONE after the other.

Holy hell, she's fucking gorgeous.

And then, shit ... I'm going to get fucking fired my first day on the job and my first week back in town.

Heat rushes down my neck and I couldn't give two shits about the latter thought. Aubrey is right on the other side of that door, frantically apologizing as if it's her fault I busted in on her.

"I apologize, Bree, I didn't mean to intrude," I call out, feeling like a fucking idiot. My hand covers my face. How is it possible that I have messed up today so badly?

I thought I was gentle enough, but it swung right open, without a single protest, revealing the woman of my dreams dressed exactly how I want her. In not a single scrap of clothing.

My splayed hand braces me against the wall to the right of her bedroom. It takes everything in me not to bang my head against the wall in frustration. Fucking hell.

With the clipboard in my left hand, I struggle to get out a single word or think of anything other than that glimpse that wasn't meant for me.

I'm hard as a fucking rock and there's no way in hell that's going to change any time soon. There's a faint sound of a drawer opening and closing behind the shut door as she calls out, "Just a minute!"

Standing up straight, I clear my throat and do my job.

Grimacing, I answer, "I just needed you to sign." Looking down, my grip is white knuckled on the clipboard and I'm surprised I didn't crack the thing in half.

Just below that, the outline of my cock is pressed against my jeans and zipper.

As she nears the door, calling out that she's

coming, I'm quick to readjust and deal with the discomfort.

The door opens and there she is in a simple and casual shirt dress. Her skin is still flushed, she's seemingly out of breath, and as she looks up at me, she tucks a lock of hair behind her ear.

The first thought I have is that she'd look better in one of my dress shirts … or it would look better on the floor.

Aubrey smiles, a bright and bashful grin as her cheeks turn red, as if she can read my mind.

Clearing my throat again, I offer her the clipboard.

"Sorry about that, I didn't see anything."

"Oh yeah?" she says as she takes the clipboard, scribbling her name down and not looking back at me. "Is that why you're looking at me like that?"

"Like what?"

"Like you saw me naked."

"I truly am apologet—"

"And like you'd like to see me like that again," she murmurs. The confidence of her previous statement is dampened and her doe eyes don't stay on mine for more than a half second before she looks down at the clipboard, holding it out with both hands for me to take back.

And there I stand, like a fool, hesitating to take the form back from her. The moment I do, I leave. That's my job.

But I'd be lying if I said I wanted this to end that way.

Aubrey

I don't know how my arms are so steady as I hold out the thin clipboard. My heart is like a wild animal in my chest, desperate to get out. I'm sure he knows how nervous I am. I imagine my face is cherry red at this point.

"Again, I didn't mean—" he murmurs, his steely eyes pinning me in place so I can't look away. The rough timbre of his voice sends a shiver of want down my spine.

"You called me Bree." I can't help that the comment falls between us, cutting him off and bringing up old times. "Just like you used to," I add quietly, barely a whisper.

I'm all too aware of the tension. It's palpable as it surrounds us.

He could stop it, I could too. I imagine if I pushed the clipboard into his chest and turned around, retreating to my bedroom and closing the door, I'd be met with a rush of cool air that would rid this lust-filled haze that's come over me.

But there's not an ounce of me that wants that.

My feet stay firmly planted and when his hand wraps around the clipboard, his thumb brushes against my skin. It's instant fire. He keeps it there, not making any effort at all to take the signed form from me.

It's not the first time his hand brushed against mine but the last time was senior year. I vaguely recall blaming the heat I felt from the innocent moment on underage drinking and overactive hormones. The music that blared seemed to fade into the background, and everything stilled. But I passed him as quickly as I could in the hallway of a friend's house and avoided him the rest of the night.

This time, though, we're not kids. There's nothing to blame for this tension.

And my bed is only feet away.

"I think—" His gaze drops from mine to my lips before the words slip from his own. "Fuck it," he murmurs and leans forward, landing a single kiss. His lips mold to mine and my back arches, deepening our touch.

Fire lights up every nerve ending in me. He steps forward, a hand on my waist, guiding me to the wall beside my door. My back hits the flat surface and he kisses me again. A mewl escapes me as my breasts press against him and a warmth builds between my legs.

I've never felt so needy in my life. I nearly say it, I nearly admit to this man what he does to me.

He's been gone for years, yet in one moment he's back and I'm weak for him. His stubble drags up my neck as he leaves openmouthed kisses, trailing up to the shell of my ear where he whispers. His warm breath leaves goosebumps down my shoulder and pebbles my already hard nipples.

"Tell me you want me to fuck you right here."

"Right here?" I echo, teasing him as I rest my head against the wall and stare up at him. I don't know how I have it in me to do anything other than beg him to have his way with me. There isn't a part of me that wants to prolong this moment, yet I stare back at him with equal desire and let my hand glide over the fabric of his shirt. My fingers slip under the hem easily and run through a smattering of chest hair. His masculine scent consumes me as he leans in closer.

My own chest rises and falls chaotically with each unsteady breath.

"For fuck's sake, Bree," he murmurs, wrapping a hand around mine and steadying it against him. "Right here, right fucking now."

The words slip out without conscious consent and I tell him, "Fuck me wherever you want." I'm barely finished saying the words before the clipboard drops to the ground and Bennet's hands have pinned me to the wall. His lips are hungrily pressed to mine.

A gasp escapes as he engulfs every inch of me.

His large hands cup my ass and the moment I'm aware of the contact, I'm lifted in his arms. Holding on to his shoulders, I let out a short chuckle of surprise but I'm instantly cut off. His hand wraps around the back of my neck, his other arm bracing me as he devours me, leaving no room for amusement. The only teasing done is by his cock rocking against my heat. My eyes widen as I realize he's hard and the way he's pressed against me, he feels massive.

I'm brought to the ground, laid on my back and given a moment to breathe. As he pulls his shirt over his head, I unbutton my dress and slide it off, revealing the lacy set beneath it. His eyes darken with lust the moment he sees me laid bare beneath him.

My heart pounds in anticipation as his gaze rakes down my body, then back up.

I can barely breathe as he braces a hand on either side of my hips and commands me to remove the rest. My bra is first. All he does is watch, his gaze hungry and his breath quickening. It's only then I see just how built Bennet is. His large shoulders are curved with muscle. His arms corded and his chest divine. He's the epitome of a tanned sex god. Tall, dark and handsome never did him justice. The man is ripped like a hunter and staring back at me like I'm his prey.

"And these," he says, his intense stare lowering to between my legs. With a single finger, he drags his touch up the center of my core and commands, "Off."

As I slip the lacy panties down my thighs, he stays right where he is, towering over me, telling me to go slower and kissing along my curves as I move. As my breasts near his face, he sucks a nipple into his mouth and that bit of contact is everything.

The pleasure, the cool air against it when he's done … fucking everything.

He teases me with peppered kisses, keeping our physical contact limited to those brief touches. It's too much yet, at the same time, not enough.

"Spread your legs for me," he murmurs while impatience takes over. I yelp as his broad shoulders push my legs apart wider and he buries his head between my thighs. He angles me, grips my tender flesh and takes a languid taste from my opening all the way up my folds. There's zero hesitation on his part and the sound of pure delight vibrates up his chest.

His tongue flicks against my clit and the sudden contact makes my back bow and my hips buck. With his hand splayed on my stomach, he keeps me where he wants me, forcing me to stay still.

His eyes peer up at me as he confesses with a barely contained grin, "You have no idea how long I have waited to taste you."

He doesn't give me a chance to respond, and thank fuck for that because this man wanting me is enough to leave me speechless. As he massages his tongue against my clit, I'm barely aware that he's undone his jeans and kicked them off. It's only as I cry out in pleasure, my fingers slipping through his dark hair as I rock myself against him, that I catch him stroking himself. With his large hand wrapped around his length, the size of him is intimidating. His hand rolls over the head of his cock and my mouth parts slightly as my bottom lip drops.

Holy fuck.

He sucks my clit and I writhe beneath him until small pleas slip from me, begging him to fuck me. I can't help it. With my neck arched back and pleasure rippling through me, all I want is for him to slam inside of me and take me exactly how I always wanted him to.

And in a single movement, it's exactly what he does. Filling me, stretching me and pinning me beneath him as he waits for me to adjust to his size.

"Fuck, Bree," he groans in unadulterated satisfaction and I lose all composure. My head falls against the floor and he takes advantage of my position to kiss my neck. He drags his teeth down my sensitized skin, one hand working my breasts, kneading them, pinching and plucking my hardened peaks. The other slips down between us and he ruthlessly rubs my clit. Without mercy and ignoring my gasps as pleasure builds in my lower stomach.

Every thrust pushes deeper inside of me, giving

a hint of pain that's quickly drowned out by the overwhelming ecstasy. It rises and rises, and a cold sweat breaks out along my skin.

"You feel so fucking good," he murmurs and I'm silent, unable to respond as it all paralyzes me.

My nails dig into his skin as my release courses through me and my heels dig into his ass. My toes curl and my back arches as waves consume me. All the while Bennet thrusts harder and faster, chasing his own release and heightening mine.

I'm brought to a second climax, this one coming faster and harder than the first before I can even catch my breath.

He groans against the crook of my neck as he loses himself. I feel every pulse of him inside of me and it only prolongs my pleasure.

As I lay there limp beneath him, the reality slowly slips in. Oh my God, what did we just do? I try not to think of it, I try to play it off before he can even say anything.

Out of breath and flushed, I hand him his shirt and then reach for my dress, covering myself.

"So eager you didn't even make it to the bed," I tease.

With his fingers on my chin, he tilts my head

up so I'm staring back into his steely gaze. There's a moment, a flicker of something between us that forces everything in me to still except my racing heart. He smirks, letting the rough pad of his thumb trail over my bottom lip and it's then that I realize, he knows exactly what he does to me. His deep cadence teases back, "How about we take it there next time?"

chapter
Five

Bennet

IT'S NOT EVERY DAY YOU RISK YOUR JOB AND a fresh start at life to sleep with an old crush. My lips kick up as my keys jingle and I unlock my front door to the ranch house I'm renting from Steve until I find my feet here back home on steady ground. The crickets are out and other than the sound of Derek's car driving off, their chirps fill up the night.

A few beers in at the bar with the guys and I finally told them I might be seeing someone. Might be. But I wouldn't say who. All because of one thing she said as I was on my way out.

The door pushes open and I flick the light on, kicking off my boots and still feeling the buzz of both beer and Bree.

Her blush, her simper, the way her hand laid flat against my chest as she got up on her tiptoes to kiss me sweetly before scooting me out the door.

"Don't tell anyone," she whispered, those gorgeous light blue eyes peering up at me. That one little comment as I pulled open the front door has lingered all night.

From the time I left, to right freaking now. I don't get why no one can know.

I've never been anyone's secret and all night long at the bar, I had to restrain myself from asking my friends about her.

What she's been doing … who she's been doing.

Reaching in my back pocket I pull out my phone before it burns a hole there. She has my number and I have hers, and eight hours since leaving her house, she hasn't texted me.

The Bree I used to know was sweet and smart, talkative with a contagious laugh. Everything feels right, but that one little statement is so far off from how I remember her.

Why should we be a secret? The thought nibbles at me from the back of my head as I make my way upstairs, kick open my bedroom door and undress.

All the while staring at my phone and remembering the details of the day.

How her back arched and the way her nails dragged down my back.

Fuck. I'm hard again just thinking about her. Everything feels just like it did before—fucking puppy love.

Tossing my clothes on top of the pile of dirty laundry in the corner of the room, I note that the room still smells of fresh paint, even if it is just a plain white shade. Other than my dresser, the TV on top of it, and my king-size bed, there are only stacks of cardboard boxes in here. The blinds are the cheap plastic kind and they look like it, since three of the slats are bent.

There's no way in hell I'm bringing Bree back here until I can fix it up. Or move out to a place of my own.

Running a hand down the back of my neck and then up over my head, all I can wonder is if I am seeing her, or if Bree just wanted to scratch an itch that's been a long time coming.

The thought is unsettling. I've wanted her for as long as I can remember and I know we went on two separate paths in life, but that doesn't change the fact that I'm back home now and that if I could have what happened today happen every damn day for the rest of my life, I'd take it.

Hell, I'd do anything to have that fire between us, that tension and built-up need.

My phone buzzes and I huff a laugh as I read it: *So who is she?*

Derek won't quit. At first he thought I was fucking around and I just didn't want to hook up with the girls at the end of the bar. He bought them a round and I did my best to be his wingman, but it caught him off guard that my first week back I met someone.

I know I know her, don't I? Derek texts and I joke back: *It's your mom.*

Not funny, he answers and then I tell him: *She wants to keep it on the downlow.*

The bed groans as I climb in, pick up the remote and turn the TV on to whatever channel it was on last. I debate on confiding in him that it might have been a one-time thing. But there's a possessive side of me that knows damn well that's not going to happen.

I want her, she wants me … I just need to make it clear to her that what happened today is damn sure going to happen again, and again, and again.

My phone goes off and I casually pick it up, expecting Derek to give me shit, but it's not Derek.

You didn't text. As Aubrey's text comes through, the name I plugged in for her brings a smile back: Bree Baby. Before I can text anything back she adds:

I thought today was wonderful btw. Especially what you did with your tongue.

Goddamn. *I don't remember you having such a dirty mouth*, I text back, my dick hardening yet again. I palm it through the sheets and readjust only for her to reply: *Ha! I knew that would get you to text me.*

A rough chuckle leaves me and I message: *In all honesty I was prepared to text back that I was just getting ready to message you. Been out all day.*

As she's typing, the three little dots informing me that she is, I add: *Been thinking about that mouth of yours and what I plan to do to it next.*

Aubrey: *No sexting just yet. That requires three dates.*

Smirking at her response I debate on what to say next. I don't want to fuck it up, but I damn sure need her to know we are in fact a thing and I will be telling this whole damn town just that.

Bennet: *Is three dates what it takes to call you my girl?*

She starts typing, then stops and all the while I lean back, sitting up in the bed, TV on although I don't have a clue what's playing. I glance at my phone, wondering what the hell is going through that pretty little head of hers.

Aubrey: *I take that to mean you don't sleep with every customer you service?*

A hum of humor leaves me as I text back: *Service? Is that what they call it now?*

Before she can second-guess a thing or starts wondering if I'm seeing other people I write: *I prefer exclusivity and it's only been you.*

I almost add to the end of the line: *since I've been back.* Almost, but it doesn't feel right. I know it's been years and I've been with people just like she has. But there's not a woman I'm interested in other than Bree.

Hell, I think fate set us up. I think she's always been meant to be mine.

After a moment she messages: *I liked you servicing me today.*

I joke, texting: *I could come back and service you right now if you'd like.* I can imagine her laugh. That sweet sound I remember so well.

Aubrey: *Calm down there, Bennet ... we might have started fast but can we take it slow?*

I second-guess my first response, which is to joke about going slow during foreplay. There's something about her that's vulnerable and I'll be damned if I fuck this up. My answer is simple: *I can go slow. We can go as slow as you want, Bree.*

A moment passes and then another of her typing a message. I imagine it's going to be long judging by the way the three dots drop out of sight and reappear, but all it is when she finally sends it is: *Tell me something I don't know.*

I rattle off a few things that have happened since I moved back. Nothing heavy and everything easy. She asks questions and I ask them back.

And there's plenty to ask.

We barely even spoke back then in high school. We were close for a short while, then it was dangerous territory, then it was nothing. Like I never existed.

I knew everything about her, and she knew everything about me. That's what happens when you live in a small town. But still we spend the entire night texting the details that this small town doesn't know about us. The little things and the big things. Until my eyelids are heavy and she tells me she has to sleep.

That's when I tell her to dream of me.

chapter
Six

Aubrey

THE PORCH SWING HAS A SUBTLE CREAK with every rock backward. Although you can hardly hear it over Marlena's laugh. Gemma doesn't stop her story as my friends on Cedar Lane continue the tradition of Wine Down Wednesday on Marlena's porch. Lauren pours another glass of sangria and Gemma downs her rosé before heading inside to get another bottle.

From here I can see my house across the street and three doors to the right. That bright blue door stares back at me. It knows my secret. I kissed Bennet on the other side of that door and not a soul knows it.

"Whatever it is, I want to know because it's got her all flustered," Gemma says in a tone that demands my attention and I look back to my left to see all three of my friends staring back expectantly.

The light is setting over the scenic view of our suburban street ... but my stomach refuses to settle down.

"What?" I try to play it off and my voice is too high pitched. Swallowing thickly, I watch Gemma's brow raise in skepticism; all the while Marlena covers her mouth to keep in a laugh. She's never been good at hiding her expressions. Add in a half pitcher of Lauren's sangria, which I swear is all alcohol because she refuses to share the recipe, and Marlena's got no hope in the world of hiding anything from us.

"Well, spill," she presses, her voice giddy with delight as she leans back in the white wicker chair. The porch swing creaks again when Lauren takes her seat next to me. This time everyone hears before she gestures for me to do the same: to spill it.

My three neighbors who I've been friends with for nearly my entire life, and even closer to these last four years I've lived on this street wouldn't tell a soul ... I don't think.

Yet my nerves rattle as my gaze moves from Marlena's gray sweats and white tee to Lauren's silk blouse she's still got on from work, to Gemma's cotton sundress. I'd rather look at their clothes than their eyes while I debate on keeping what happened yesterday a secret.

"Is it something bad?" Lauren's tone turns concerned.

"No, no, no," I answer quickly before gulping down the last bit of sangria and deciding to just do it. To tell them what happened.

"You remember Bennet, right?" I say.

Marlena's eyes go wide before she shrieks with glee. "I knew it! You got laid!" Heat floods my cheeks. "Nuh-uh," Lauren says doubtfully but when I don't look back at her and attempt to have another sip only to find the etched glass empty, she gasps. With a light slap on my arm, she says, "You didn't?"

For a very small moment, I don't hear the humor or the happiness of a friend excited for another friend. I hear an ounce of dread or betrayal, like we're all back in high school and I just slept with Pamela's ex.

Lauren's next comment erases those thoughts just as quickly as her gasp put them there. "He is so freaking hot." She adds, "When did he even get back to town?"

"He came in last week or the week before I think."

I nod along as Gemma answers and work on calming my racing heart.

"And you and him banged?" Lauren asks.

"Banged?" A deep crease settles in her forehead as Marlena looks at Lauren and asks, "Who calls it 'bang?'"

"The horizontal tango, scratched an itch, fornicated, fooled around, went all the way—who cares what you call it? There are only two questions that matter," Gemma states, gathering our attention as the sun sets a little deeper and she stares at me with a serious expression. "One, was it good, and two, how big is he?"

Lauren and Marlena howl and I have to laugh at the ridiculousness.

I bring my empty glass up to my lips as if I could hide behind it but then hold it with both hands in my lap. I'm already in my pajamas because I have every intention of climbing into bed the moment I waddle my tipsy butt back to my house.

I tell them, "It was good and," my smile grows as I add, "he is very blessed."

Another round of shrieks and laughs consumes the porch and this time Miss Margaret, an older woman who takes long walks around the block in the evening, hears us as she's walking past. I catch her eye just as she's staring at us while shaking her head in mock disappointment, but she's smiling the entire time. Margaret keeps it moving in her joggers and I give her a wave, letting the warmth run through me.

"He's the one Pamela dated, right?" Gemma asks and Marlena nods as she replies, "For a few months, I think in eleventh grade?"

"We don't need to talk about her right now." Lauren cuts off their conversation as they remember all the details they can about Bennet. "Pamela has a husband and a third baby on the way. She got her happily ever after and now it's time," Lauren looks back at me, "for Aubrey to tell us exactly how big he is."

Her joke breaks up the small bit of tension that's brewing in the pit of my stomach.

The secret is out, and nerves prick their way down my shoulders.

"Yesterday he came over, I just got out of the shower, looked a mess ... then some things just ... happened."

"He's working for Stew, right?" Gemma asks and I nod.

"So he came over to unclog your pipes?" Lauren

jokes and then she laughs, but Marlena doesn't take her eyes off me.

"So you saw him just yesterday and you two hit it off?" There's no judgment there, but there is a note of worry in her tone. Like it's a recipe for disaster.

"Yup," I answer and set the glass down before crossing my legs on the porch swing and readjusting.

Lauren keeps it rocking and asks, "Was it a fling?"

"I don't think so," I say.

"So you like him," Gemma teases and my smile comes back.

All I can do is nod. I really, really like him. I don't tell them we stayed up last night talking until the early morning. I don't tell them he brings back butterflies and all kinds of hope I haven't had in years.

"So … are you two dating then?" Marlena asks, her smile ready to widen. The moment I answer, the girls squeal with delight and I'm forced to smile and feel at ease.

"I think so."

chapter
Seven

Aubrey

AN EDITOR DOESN'T NEED TO WEAR A lace bralette and high-waisted, wide-legged pants. She certainly doesn't need to wear heels in her own home after all the meetings of the day are over. Not that I wore this getup for the meetings. My heel tap, tap, taps as I sit perched on the bottom step, waiting for the knock at the front door with my phone in my hands.

I text Bennet that the microwave stopped working earlier today and he said he'd come by and see what he could do.

There may have been some flirtatious banter

with him hinting I could pay him with dinner and me offering up *dessert* as an extra incentive.

As it stands, my microwave works just fine. Just like how yesterday the dishwasher was just fine and the fridge the day before that.

It's been four days in a row and yet the butterflies don't quit.

Knock, knock.

I bite my lip to keep the smile at bay as I pop up from where I was sitting and go to my front door.

It swings open and reveals my handsome man in a dress shirt and slacks with a bottle of red wine. Plus a steely gaze that falls down my body hungrily and shamelessly.

His brow rises with surprise and he says, "You look fucking incredible."

"I was going to say the same to you," I answer in appreciation. His stubble is just right and I can already feel it gently scratching the crook of my neck as he takes me again tonight.

I can't help the sweet hint of soreness that comes from clenching my thighs at the thought or the blush that rises to my cheeks.

He sees it and I'm not sure if it's the blush or

the clenching, but either way he grins as he steps inside, leaving the dusk of the spring night to fall behind us.

He stops at the sight of Chinese food lined up on the counter, plates already set. In the last week we've practically shared every trivia question imaginable about each other and I know lo mein and pepper steak are his favorite.

"I thought maybe I could feed you for your trouble."

As he's staring at dinner, I take the bottle of wine from him with both hands and make my way to the cabinet for the wine opener. "Oh, it's a miracle by the way," I tell him, looking over my shoulder as I reach up and notice how he's watching my ass. "The microwave seems just fine now." I smirk at him and he just shakes his head.

"You're going to run out of appliances soon, Bree baby," he murmurs, standing right where he is, staring at me in a way that only makes me hot.

Bree baby. My body heats at that little nickname he has for me. He's got me flustered most of the day, but come night and I'm a wreck just for him. So much so, I set the first glass down a little too hard. It doesn't break but it's loud and I let out a little gasp.

"You need help?" he asks and doesn't wait for an answer, coming up behind me, his chest to my back, an arm on either side of me. He lowers his lips to the shell of my ear and then teases me, "Next thing you know, you're going to break the wine opener and it will be a real emergency for me to come over."

With a gentle laugh, I ease back into him. Even though he seems dead set on opening that bottle of wine, I reach up splaying my fingers through his hair and lock my lips on his. His chest rumbles against my back as he groans in satisfaction, sweeping his tongue across the seam of my lips, urging me to part them for him and I do. Eagerly and hungrily, I deepen the kiss and ignore the click of the wine opener falling on the counter as I turn in his arms and let the kiss consume me.

The kiss and touch I've been thinking about all day.

It's everything I've always dreamed of. I'm starting to think he may really be my happily ever after.

These feelings are dangerous. To know you're falling and not want to stop … that's how you set yourself up for heartbreak. And yet, as I fall back into his embrace, I'd willingly hand over whatever Bennet wanted. If he keeps holding me, kissing me, and wanting me like he does, I would give him whatever he asked for.

"Bree," he says and breathes between us.

"Yeah, I'm going to need you to keep these heels on while I fuck you tonight," he murmurs in the crook of my neck before lifting me in his arms. Letting out a squeal, I can't help smiling into his shoulder as he nips the lobe of my ear, carrying me into the living room and never stopping the kisses along my neck.

༄

Bennet

Her curves are tempting, her amused gasps and lust-filled moans addictive, but it's that look in her eyes that gets me every time. Her vulnerability mixed with desire. She gives all of herself to me and I can't get enough. I'm drunk on her every night and I wouldn't have it any other way.

With an arm bracing her back, I lay her down

on the sofa and she's already started undressing herself. I love it when she takes it slow, but hell, I've wanted her all damn day so she can rip off these clothes if she'd like. Still, kissing down her neck I tease her by asking, "Needy tonight, aren't you?"

She writhes under me and I watch goosebumps travel down her shoulder from my peppered kisses. Her nipples are already hard and I waste no time moving to them, sucking as I knead her breasts.

Her inhale is sharp and her legs spread easily for me as I go about devouring every inch of her. I have to help her pull her pants off as she lifts her ass off the sofa, careful to keep those heels in place. The sofa groans as I stand up to undress, kicking off my shoes first while I stare down at her. A gorgeous delight with fuck-me heels and doe eyes.

Damn, how did I get so lucky?

With her teeth sinking into her bottom lip she leans forward to unbutton my dress slacks and I let her take control, watching her as she takes my already hard cock out and licks along my slit. A shiver runs up my spine with the teasing touch.

I let her play, hollowing her cheeks and sucking me down, taking me in deeper and deeper until the head of my cock is pressed against the back of her throat.

"Fuck, Bree," I groan before letting my head fall back. The sight of her and the feel of her warm mouth are going to get me off if I don't take control.

"Lay down and spread your legs for me," I command and she's eager to obey. Her lips are swollen already and a gorgeous cherry color as she lays back. Exactly how I want her.

With two fingers I play with her slit, spreading her arousal to her clit and rubbing there teasingly. "Already wet for me," I tease her.

"Mm-hmm," she murmurs.

"You need me to fuck you, Bree?"

"Yes." She barely manages the single word as I strum faster. She could come undone just like this. I make it faster, though, slipping two fingers inside of her, curving them and finger fucking her with my palm pressed against her clit with each deep stroke.

Her back arches as she protests the sudden onslaught of pleasure. A strangled cry is muffled as she bites down on her lower lip. Her hips rock and I know she's close.

"Come on my hand like I've been dreaming

about all fucking day," I command, a hand on her lower stomach pinning her hip down, holding her in place and intensifying the quickened strokes.

She comes almost instantly, like she was waiting for permission.

I don't pull away at first, I keep up the pressure on her clit until she remembers how to breathe and looks back at me with those pale blue eyes full of lust.

Then I climb between her legs, line up my cock, and fuck her into her sofa until she's clinging to me, out of breath and completely sated.

chapter
Eight

Bennet

"I COULD SEE A FIREPLACE RIGHT THERE," I comment as I run my fingers up and down Bree's bare shoulder.

She turns slightly in my arms from where she is on the sofa and her tired expression brightens. "Before I even bought this house I thought that. I've always wanted one."

"I could build you one," I offer and it dawns on me that I would stop the world tomorrow to build her whatever she wanted.

Her doe eyes peer up at me and she gives me the sweetest simper. "I may have to make a handyman call for that one of these days then," she half jokes although there's nothing about her gaze that holds humor.

Choosing to let it be, I turn my attention back to the show neither of us are watching. This late at night, with the empty takeout boxes still on the table, both of us are doing what we've been doing: pretending not to be dog tired just so we can stay up a little longer together.

Her back to my front, cuddled up and lying down on the sofa.

I kiss her shoulder and smirk when she shivers like I knew she would. Whispering, I tell her, "I've got to get going, baby."

She hums in protest with a pout, but pushes away the small throw blanket like she's going to get up.

"Where's your wrench?" she asks me before holding back a yawn. I see it, though. She adds before I can answer, "I'm going to go break something."

A rough chuckle leaves me and her face lights up with that gorgeous smile.

"That smirk of yours is wicked," I tell her and she blushes. I fucking love what I do to her ... and what she does to me.

The days are bleeding together and if there's one

thing I'd like to change, it's this part right here. The part where I give her a goodnight kiss and leave.

There's not a part of me that doesn't want to lay her to sleep in bed, like her man should.

Like I should.

⤴

Aubrey

I don't think I've ever wanted someone in my bed overnight. Not a moment has existed where I've thought: *I'd like to share and I definitely won't regret not being able to cocoon myself in my comforter or spawl out.* But every night he leaves, there's an emptiness I can't shake.

When I lie down, I imagine what it would be like to share the bed with him and sleep soundly in his arms. My eyes close as the front door shuts and that's all I see: the image of the two of us, sleeping together. Actually sleeping.

Peeking out of the peephole, I watch him take his time walking to his car. He peers over his shoulder, looking back with his keys in his hand and I know he can't see me, but I wish he could.

If he could, I think he'd ask if I want him to stay.

He lingers more and more each time he leaves and the invitation is on the tip of my tongue. Taking a step back, I let out a deep breath and cross my arms over my chest. I know how it will happen, though.

He stays a night, maybe a couple in a row.

And then either we're sick of each other and need space, or it's a full-blown "come move in with me" situation.

I'm not sure which way it'll go and my nerves eat away at me, dreading that if we move to that next step, it could lead to a split. That's the last thing I want, but I don't think I can stand here one more time and watch him leave me.

I don't know what it is about tonight, but my heart pounds and I can't just stay here, pacing in my foyer, thinking about all the what-ifs.

I'll never know if I don't take the leap.

Ripping open the door, I ready myself to run out in the dark night lit only by the full moon and stop him. To call out his name, hoping he sees and hears me before he drives off.

I'm so prepared and determined that when I open the door, I'm shocked to see him standing there on the bottom step, keys in his hands still, with a look in his eyes that tells me he's just as shocked.

My heart rages and my body heats as he smirks up at me and says, "Bree baby?"

"Did you leave something?" I question him breathlessly, wondering why he came back.

"I think I did." His charming smile widens and he slips his hands into his dress slacks as he stands a few steps away. "Did you have something you needed to … say or ask?" he questions and I swear I've never been more in love. The ease between us, the look in his eyes. There's a spark I pray never goes away.

"Stay the night?"

"Isn't that a little serious?" he asks in a playful tone, taking a single step forward, but still too far away for my liking. I venture a step outside, standing under the porch light.

"I think I could be serious with you."

"You're not afraid of falling in love with me, Bree baby?"

"I think I already am." Before the words are fully spoken his arms are wrapped around me and his lips are on mine, stealing the gasp. He kisses me in the light spilling from my front door, for all of Cedar Lane to see.

Epilogue

Aubrey

I DON'T WAKE UP FEELING SO ALONE, SO MUCH anymore. Even though I am.

No longer dreaming of Bennet, I reach over to the cold sheets where he used to lay. Where he kissed me a thousand times and where he held me in the darkest moments of our lives. Before we were torn apart.

Every night, though, I see him again. As if it's a decade ago and when we first met all over again.

I don't know much about soulmates or fate or whether the vows we made on our wedding day meant anything past the moment he left me, but every night I dream of my husband. Only I don't know him. It's as if we're complete strangers who fall hard for each other. The days are lonely and he's not here to tell me it's all right … but when I sleep, we get to start over from the beginning and I feel those butterflies anew. We have our first kiss and I am loved again. I miss him every waking moment and, in my dreams, we re-live our romance as if it's the first time. Every single night, I fall in love with him all over again.

Bennet

In *our* dreams, my love.

I see you and I miss you too.

But at least I have you at night.

This is not the end …

The Fall in Love Again series will feature Bennet and Bree falling in love on the small-town fictional street of Cedar Lane over and over again while the real world has had other plans for them. Because love is endless and this is what forever means. In any and every life, their love was meant to be. And there's so much to tell in the dreams where they get to meet again for the first time every night.

More to come in the Fall in Love Again series, oming to Patreon exclusively:

Even in Our Dreams (book 2)
A Night with You (book 3)

about the
Author

Thank you so much for reading my romances. I'm just a stay at home mom and avid reader turned author and I couldn't be happier.

I hope you love my books as much as I do!

More by Willow Winters

WWW.WILLOWWINTERSWRITES.COM/BOOKS

Made in the USA
Middletown, DE
09 June 2023

31860186R00047